TOOTH FAIRY KILLER,

a Mary MacIntosh novel

MAUREEN ANNE MEEHAN

TOOTH FAIRY KILLER,

Copyright © 2024 by Maureen Anne Meehan

ISBN: 979-8-3481-6757-8

E-book ISBN: 979-8-3481-6758-5

www. maureenmeehanbooks.com

info@maureenmeehan.com

Table of Contents

AUTHOR'S NOTE

This novel was difficult to write. My family has a tradition of dentistry, law, and creative arts. The concept of a serial killer harming righteous families is hard to endure. It is challenging to write it based on my own personal losses. I was bullied massively as a child, my legal secretary was brutally murdered, and my soulmate husband passed away from cancer, leaving me to raise four teens.

But we endure and strive to overcome our challenges. God is good. God only gives us what makes us stronger. Faith. Family. Friendship. Financial Responsibility. Loyalty. These are my five non-negotiables.

I pray to meet a partner who has these qualities. I pray that you do as well.

DEDICATION

This novel is dedicated to the families who were victims of the Tooth Fairy Killer, namely, the Jacobi family of Birmingham, Alabama, and the Leeds family of Atlanta, Georgia.

It is also dedicated to the hard investigatory work of Will Graham of the FBI. Will took down Hannibal Lecter, but not without a life-threatening injury.

It is also dedicated to the love interest of the Tooth Fairy Killer, Reba McClane, who showed this man affection, attention, and love. She is likely the reason he stopped killing families and despising women.

It is also dedicated to the CEO of United HealthCare, Brian Thompson.

Chapter 1

The woman is a symbol of purity, divine grace, and the Church. She is described as being crowned with stars, with the moon under her feet, and clothed in the sun's light. She represents the ultimate good and creation, contrasting with the evil destruction of the devil. The battle between good and evil, God and the devil, and the woman equates to a battle as the woman is a cosmic struggle between good and evil.

In Birmingham, Alabama, an evil man named leaves behind his first known victims. The entire family has been brutally slaughtered. The killer leaves behind no survivors, and the crime scene shows evidence of ritualistic posing of the victims. The FBI has no clue as to who this killer is and there is little DNA evidence left behind. However, the killer has bitten each member of the family and has left behind his teeth marks, denoting crooked, jagged teeth and a narrow jaw.

The killer has broken every mirror in the house and has used shards of glass from the broken mirrors to dig out the victims' eyeball which he had taken as a token. In place of each victim's eyeballs remained the shards of glass.

The first family killed is the Jacobi family in Birmingham, Alabama.

The victims were staged in the parents' master bedroom and mom and dad brutally bloodied on their bed, with the three children who were killed in their respective bedrooms, dragged to the master and posed to sit upright and stare at the dead parents. All had shards of glass protruding from their empty eye sockets as if they were watching this brutal murder through their mirrored eyes.

No one in this quaint, quiet residential neighborhood has seen or heard a thing. There is no motive that could be uncovered, as the family was of model citizen stature. The father was a successful, hard-working businessman and the mother was saintly in her roles as wife, mother, and caretaker of the home. The children were good students and were not troublemakers.

The only clue is the calling card of the bite marks left behind.

There was no sign of a break-in, no sign of a struggle, and the family dog was nowhere to be seen. No one heard a dog bark. No one saw or heard anything.

It was like a ghost snuck into this home and committed gruesome, ritualistic murders, with no motive. The local, state and federal law enforcement teams were baffled. The FBI sent several serial killer profilers to investigate.

One profiler was none other than the man who put Hannibal Lecter behind bars – Will Graham.

He worked in conjunction with the FBI profiling team, including John Douglas who was famous for his work on the Zodiac Killer case from the San Francisco Bay Area in the 1960s and 1970s, a case that to this day remains cold.

Not one of these experts had a clue as to why this crime happened.

Chapter 2

Within months of the Jacobi family murders in Birmingham, Alabama, another family is found in a similarly staged crime scene in Atlanta, Georgia. The Leeds family of four was remarkably similar to the Jacobi family in that they were a model citizen family, with the father as a businessman, the mother as a stay-at-home mom, and the two children were good kids. They, too, were staged in the parent's bedroom with a house of broken mirrors and with shards of glass in lieu of their eyeballs. The crime scene was also brutally gruesome, and the killer left bite marks on each victim.

It didn't take forensic dentists long to determine that the bite marks were unique and exactly the same as the ones left behind on the Jacobi family. The FBI was aware that this was one serial killer, but they had absolutely no idea who it was or why. These families did not have any connection. They lived in a different state, and no member of either family had an ounce of connectivity. It seemed random. The only non-random thing was the calling card of the bite marks as well as the broken mirrors and missing eyeballs.

Whatever monster was doing this, was doing crimes with precision and premeditation.

The profilers surmised that the killer must have viewed these idealistic families as "covenants" and must have meticulously chosen his victims by stalking them to observe their routines and vulnerabilities. He obviously suffered a mental health issue and must have delusions regarding the goodness of his victims. They agreed that he had a cleft lift by the shape of his bite marks and that he was likely teased, abused, and/or neglected as a child.

Another commonality is that he killed during a full moon. The full moon seemed to dictate his schedule for selecting victims or carrying out these murders. He could have a physical or symbolic interaction with the moon – perhaps standing in its light before a crime, meditating under it, or photographing it as part of his ritual.

He typically bludgeoned or shot his victims, staging their bodies in specific, symbolic ways that align with his delusions.

The bite marks left on each victim earned him the name "Tooth Fairy" from law enforcement. His distorted teeth and the impression they left became a significant clue in the investigation.

In addition, the trophy taken from his victims was ritualistic. Taking eyeballs was highly unusual, and leaving shards of glass in their wake was unheard of.

The killer might have used the full moon as a time of ritualistic murder, believing the transformation from crescent to full moon granted him the superhuman strength of a diving connection to the stars. The FBI profilers surmised that his severe childhood trauma and his delusions of being chosen to transform into a powerful entity forced him to believe that murdering these model families and staging the crime scenes was a form of ritualistic sacrifice.

FBI special agent and profiler Will Graham believed that these crime scenes were biblical in nature and consulted with Biblicists and artists to see if there could be a connection between the ritualism with perhaps the Book of Revelation in the Bible in addition to some piece of artwork that related to this dark theme.

One such piece of art was identified as The Great Red Dragon and the Woman Clothed with the Sun, symbolizing a desire to rid a beast of its power. This piece of art depicted a monstrous entity with seven heads, ten horns, and a tail that sweeps a third of the stars from the sky. It represents evil versus chaos, rebellion against the divine order, power from transformation, rebellion against God, control over others, sexuality and obsession, and the duality of good and evil.

Perhaps the killer was obsessed with these opposing dynamics.

Chapter 3

"**L**et's discuss The Great Red Dragon and the Woman Clothed in the Sun," Will Graham said to John Douglas during a meet at the FBI headquarters in Washington, D.C. John Douglas and Will Graham had worked closely together as FBI serial-killer profilers for years and they had a great deal of mutual respect for one another.

"It's a powerful piece, I must admit," John stated.

"What does the Red Dragon represent?" Will asked, almost ceremoniously.

"In my opinion, the Red Dragon depicts a transcendent being, and I think our killer sees the Red Dragon as granting him an escape from his feelings of inadequacy, self-loathing, and childhood trauma. He believes he is 'becoming the Red Dragon' meaning that he is shedding his humanity and weakness in favor of godlike strength and invincibility," John said with confidence.

Will looked at him quizzically. "That's pretty deep for a guy like you."

"I'm quoting someone," John admitted.

"Let me guess.   Mary MacIntosh?"

"How did you know?" John said, sheepishly.

"Because I have never worked with her, but you have exclusively, and it has upped your game as a profiler massively. She thinks out of the box in a way neither of us are capable of. Her insight is alarmingly accurate," Will said.

"Truly. She sees things in colors that I may never see," John suggested.

"Let expound on her theory. If the Red Dragon represents power and transformation, then is the Red Dragon a representative of Satan or a demonic entity?" Will asked.

"Mac thinks that it represents Satan's war against God and His creations. She said that the killer is identifying with the Dragon to rebel against a world he perceives as cruel and rejecting of him," John said.

"Let's assume that the persona of the Red Dragon helps the killer seek dominance over his victims. What do you make of the ritualistic staging of the victims?"

"Mac thinks that the act of staging the scene is a ritualistic submission to the Dragon's power. She thinks that it extends to his personal life, where the struggles between the Dragon's influence and the killer's genuine desire to connect with others is causing a chasm in his psyche," John said.

"Did she get a degree in psychology?" Will asked, not knowing a lot about Mac and her background, other than the fact that she was both a defense attorney in her younger years as an associate attorney and then a prosecutor in her later years.

"As a matter of fact, she has a degree in business from undergrad, and then a master's in psychology before going to law school. She truly understands mental health issues and struggles, and easily diagnoses a crime scene using her 'sixth sense' I think," John said. "It's like her mind is four-dimensional. It analyzes crime scenes in a way I would never imagine."

"The artist who described this work to us said something about sexuality. Did you ask Mac about that?" Will said.

"She said that the Dragon embodies the killer's repressed sexual desires, which must have been twisted by his upbringing and psychological issues. His identification with the Dragon allows him to express these desires through violence."

Will scratched his chin while thinking about this "Interesting analysis," he agreed."

"She went on to tell me that she thinks the killer's inner conflict is personified by the Dragon. He alternates between being consumed by the evil influence of the Dragon versus moments of resistance where he wishes to stop killing. She said it is the quintessential battle between good and evil. He is personifying this notion."

I will take this in. "Can we get her out here to help us?" Will asked.

"I've begged her already, but she said that it is not a good time to be away from her family.

She said that her two sets of twins were embarking on their teenage years and that they needed her more than ever. And her husband, Burg, doesn't want her to travel. The situation with the Midnight Scribe murders shined too brightly on exposing their family to violence, and Burg, as a sheriff, and Mac as a former prosecutor, both feel that it's time for them to avoid danger and protect the family."

"I understand, but we need her in person to analyze this. She has more of an angle on this than we do, and she's not even working the case," Will said.

"Yes, she is," John admitted. "I received permission to engage her remotely."

"And you're just telling me this now!" Will said with a raised eyebrow and a jilted tone.

"I'm sorry, but I like to have her to myself. She teaches me more than anyone ever has during my tenure with the FBI."

"Selfish, selfish, selfish, selfish," Will teased. "Work on getting her out here in person on our team.

We have no leads and no clues other than the bite marks, and she already sees things that we haven't even considered," Will said to John.

"Believe me, I am trying to."

Chapter 4

Mary MacIntosh had served as a prosecuting attorney in Sheridan, Wyoming for years. Prior to prosecuting crimes, she was a defense attorney for both civil and criminal cases. She had a reputation as a very smart woman, excellent attorney, supportive wife, and loving mother of her two sets of twins.

Mac met her husband by accident when they were both working on a criminal case. She was prosecuting the crime, and he was a sheriff in a neighboring town. The crime spree happened in both of their jurisdictions, and they needed to consult regularly to update each other on the ever-changing facts. Burg, as he was affectionally known, was now the Sheridan Sheriff and had become so shortly after they married.

Burg had two adult daughters, and Mac never had aspirations to become a mother. Her professional life was her baby, and she didn't have a great childhood as a reference. Her father was a mean man and a member of some secret society. He abandoned Mac and her mother, Madelaine, when Mac was seven years old. She holds few good memories of her father, and her mother died young of a broken heart, in conjunction with breast cancer.

Shortly after Mac and Burg were married, Mac started feeling ill in the mornings.

She would go on her morning run early and naturally feel better by the time she got to the office. She didn't want to worry Burg, so she didn't mention it to him.

One day he asked her if she was late for her monthly, and she admitted that it was possible, but that she was on contraception, so it hadn't crossed her mind. Sure enough, she was two months pregnant with what turned out to be twin boys. She cried Burg celebrated.

Mac was overwhelmed with balancing motherhood with her life as an attorney, whereas Burg took it in stride. He was a natural father, and little things didn't get under his skin. On the contrary, Mac was a perfectionist, and she consistently felt like she was failing on all fronts. Burg assured her that she wasn't failing on any front, and with assurances, she became pregnant again within months of giving birth to the twins.

Once again, she cried, while Burg was elated. When the twin girls were born several months later, Mac was overwhelmed with four children within fifteen months, all under the age of two. The house was chaotic at all times and was often cluttered and dirty. The children were never neglected. They had two amazing parents. But not even a nanny and a housekeeper could keep up with the twins.

It drove Mac crazy. She was accustomed to neat, orderly and quiet. Their house was in utter chaos.

Burg loved it. She did not. They didn't argue about the house or messes, though. The only thing they argued over was time.

The time Mac spent working. The dangerous cases she prosecuted were another sore spot.

Burg finally convinced Mac to not run again for office as the county prosecutor when John Douglas of the FBI entered her life. He consulted with Mac on several cases that she was prosecuting, and they had become fast friends. John begged Mac to serve as a consultant to the FBI when he was profiling cases, and she readily accepted. This allowed her independence and flexibility, and she could work from home nearly full-time. The exception was when she needed to view a crime scene with John and the FBI team, but Burg put his foot down a few years back when such a consultation turned deadly toward Mac. Her life and the safety of her family were threatened, and at that point, Burg was not going to tolerate it further. Their agreement was that she would continue to consult, but from home. The family came first.

Chapter 5

"*P*lease, we beg of you," John and Will groveled to Mac. "We have absolutely nothing on this guy. People on the East Coast are freaked out by the Tooth Fairy Killer."

"I promised my family that I would stay put and consult from home," Mac said over the Zoom. "The kids are busy in school and sports and extra-curricular activities, and I am room mom and team mom and scout leader."

"Of course you are," John jested. "Overachiever."

"You were the same. Both of you."

"Fair. But you have a lot of help at home, and the kids won't miss you for a few days. It would be good for you to take a break, and it would be good for Burg to miss you a little bit," John suggested.

"He is a little possessive," Mac joked. "I swear, he follows me like a puppy still after all of these years!"

"He married up, Mac, and he is the first to brag about it," John said. John and Mac and Burg had become very close friends over the years, and John teased Burg incessantly over his tail-wagging, tongue drooping obsession with his wife.

Mac let out a gaffe. "Let me talk with Burg tonight after sports and dinner.

I already know his answer, though. This is a very violent set of crimes against families, and after our experience with the Midnight Scribe Killer, we are both reticent to let our guard down. That crazy man showed up at our house!"

"I was there, Mac. I saw it first-hand, and it was terrifying. Anyone would be freaked out by what transpired," John assured her.

"I'll talk with him, but don't get your hopes up," Mac said. "Back to the Tooth Fairy Killer. I've been analyzing the case file and as I told you, I think the woman is a symbol of purity to him, and I think he was bullied, and treated the Woman Clothed in the Sun as his way to sort out his identity. I think he wants to become the Red Dragon in a demonic way, representing evil, and attempting to destroy the woman and her child as a form of emoting Christ and purity. The Dragon's goal is to devour the child – a symbol of innocence and salvation. I think he sees himself as the child, and that his innocence was robbed of him by his mean-spirited mother."

John took a look at Will. He was shaking his head while taking notes.

"The Dragon represents chaos, domination, and rebellion against divine authority," Mac continued. "It is both terrifying and awe-inspiring. It is the ultimate power and primal rage."

"I don't have much background in theology, as my parents did not raise us with religion," John admitted. "Do either of you know much about Biblical references?

We have an expert on our team, but we both feel like he gets too deep in the weeds, and we don't really see his bigger picture."

"My mom raised me with religion. She was a bit fanatical about it after my dad left us," Mac said. "In looking at the painting by William Blake, and researching his past works of art, he maintains a good deal of theology and Biblical reference. In the Bible's Book of Revelation, the Red Dragon is depicted as Satan or a demonic entity waging a war against God. By assuming the persona of the Red Dragon, the killer seeks dominance over his victims. His crimes are staged as acts of ritualistic submission to the Dragon's power."

"How do you know this?" Will asked.

"Unlike you guys at the FBI, I don't have to go to senseless meetings in a bureaucratic agency, and therefore I have time to simply either be with the family or work. I don't have wasted time," Mac said.

I will send John a look. It went without saying that they knew she was right. Both lamented often about the meaningless conferences and meetings they were forced to attend,

"This control notion also extends to his personal life. I think he struggles between the evil forces of the Dragon and his genuine desire to connect with a loving human."

"Like a mother figure?" John asked.

"Either a mother figure or a lover, or both," Mac said. "I think the latter shows his repressed sexual desires, as you mentioned that he raped both women, correct?"

"That's what the forensics tells us," Will said. "So he is expressing his sexual desires through violence?"

"Yes."

Chapter 6

"**I** hear that you received a returned call from Hannibal Lecter," John said to Will.

"Yes. He has agreed to a meeting," Will said.

"Be careful, my friend. Hannibal Lecter would sooner kill you than help you with this Tooth Fairy Killer case. You are the agent that put him behind bars. You were the only profiler that figured out that he was the killer," John reminded Will.

"I know. My wife is freaking out on me for even considering it, but we are stuck in mud here. No further crimes, thank goodness, but no movement. I've never felt this hopelessness other than when I was trying to figure out who Hannibal was," Will admitted.

"Your wife is spot-on. I don't care if he is at the Baltimore State Hospital for the Criminally Insane."

"It's a high-security prison," Will said.

The Baltimore State Hospital for the Criminally Insane was designed to house violent and psychopathic offenders deemed mentally unfit to serve time in regular prisons. It's known for treating and containing some of the most dangerous criminals in the country. Hannibal Lecter's cell was unique for it was designed specifically for maximum security. It was made of reinforced glass instead of bars, to prevent physical interactions.

It included a minimal furnishing, including a bed, toilet, small desk, and limited reading and writing materials. His cell was in the basement of the hospital, emphasizing his status as an exceptionally dangerous patient.

The hospital was run by Dr. Frederick Chilton, a very manipulative man that Will despised. Will believed that he was incompetent, and he didn't like the way that he treated mental health patients. He felt that he was unusually cruel and treated them like animals. Will was not a softy on crime, but he strongly believed in human decency, and that rehabilitation should include treating all inmates with compassion and understanding.

This hospital enforced stringent security measures, including regular monitoring and multiple layers of locked doors, called chambers or Mods. Will did feel safe in the high-security hospital, but he was wary of the likelihood that Hannibal would try to manipulate him with his wit and intelligence. Will's wife was gravely concerned about this.

Will wanted to interview him regarding the Tooth Fairy Killer case and was told that Lecter was about to be transferred to the Tennessee courthouse for a hearing. There was no way that Will, John, or any other member of the FBI profiling team would consult with Lecter in any setting shy of the Baltimore high-security setting.

Lecter agreed to the meeting in exchange for access to more reading materials.

They agreed on a date, and Will was scheduled to meet with Lecter the following week.

Chapter 7

"**A**re you sitting down?" Mac said on the Zoom to John and Will. "I just scanned and emailed you a secure document with the 12-digit security code on your phone," Mac continued. "Open it and read it, I'll wait."

Both John and Will looked at the one-page letter. "What is this?" Will asked her.

"It's a threat," Mac said. "The Tooth Fairy Killer mailed a letter to my home threatening me now to get involved in your investigation, or he will see to it that I will never struggle again with balancing my career and family because we will all be dead in my master bedroom with mirrors for eyes!"

"Oh My God," John yelled. This sent chills down his spine, and it made Will queasy. "Did you show Burg?"

"Not yet," Mac said. I wanted to get your take on it, but I think we need FBI security at the house now. We need local, state and federal protection."

"Like the Witness Protection Program?" John asked.

"Hell no!" "Those people have to disappear. I'm not agreeing to that!"

"I'm on it," John said. You need to call Burg now and get him home. He can summon troops, and we will arrange state and federal backup."

"On it," Mac said as she left the Zoom meeting. She immediately called Burg.

She told him what had happened and forwarded the email she'd sent to John and Will to Burg's sheriff email.

"I told you not to get involved in this!" Burg shouted into the phone. It took a lot to get him angry. He was clearly angry.

"Burg, hold it together. Get troops up here. Come home," she ordered.

The line went dead. For the first time in the history of their relationship, Burg hung up on his wife.

Chapter 8

*T*he police arrived in force at Mac and Burg's home. The children were sequestered in the basement, sheltered from the swarming media. By the time Burg got home, he had calmed down a little, but he was furious with Mac for once again endangering their family and putting her career before family.

"We need to talk," Burg said to her out of the presence of the kids.

"I know," Mac said, her eyes lowered in shame.

"I think we need to separate," Burg continued.

Tears welled in both of their eyes. She knew this way was coming. She couldn't dodge this bullet, and she didn't blame him.

"I understand," she said, surrendering.

"This has happened two too many times for us to last one more day together.'

She capitulated with resignation in her voice.

"It's my fault," she admitted. "I just can't stop myself."

"You will never stop, Mac, and you know that under these circumstances, the judge will award me full custody of both sets of twins."

"I know."

"I hope this was worth it to you to lose your husband and your children in lieu of your career," John said with disgust.

"It's not worth it," Mac said.

"Obviously to you, it is. You keep doing it despite the risk. I don't get the risk-reward analysis going on in that bright brain of yours, but the numbers don't add up for a wife and mother of four," Burg said. She could see anger seething in his eyes.

"These cases are like a bad drug for me," Mac admitted.

"These cases are your cocaine. Moms on cocaine don't get to keep their children," Burg continued.

"I know," she admitted. "I don't deserve them. I love them to the moon and back," Mac said, "but I don't deserve them."

"No. You don't. And you don't deserve a faithful, honest, loving husband either," he continued.

"You are right," she said while letting out a large sigh.

"You will be moving out today. I will help you pack," Burg said, as he headed upstairs to their master closet. "Pack up your office and I will pack your clothes, and I will have one of my deputies drive you to a hotel of your choosing, hopefully on the opposite end of town.

As she watched the man of her dreams walk away, she pivoted to pack her computer and files. This was happening. It was real. She was being forced to leave the family home and say goodbye to the best things that had ever happened to her.

Chapter 9

*A*s Mac unpacked her suitcases and boxes in her hotel room at The Historic Sheridan Inn, she couldn't abate the flow of tears streaming down her cheeks. She wished that she had done a better job as a wife and a mother, and she wished that she had been better at staying in touch with friends. Her career had always come before relationships, and it was punishing her now because she had no one to call for a good cry on their shoulders.

Her room was spacious and comfortable as the hotel, located in downtown Sheridan, Wyoming is historic and known for its Western charm and connection to Buffalo Bill Cody, who once co-owned the establishment. Earnest Hemmingway stayed there as well and wrote a portion of A Farewell to Arms while staying as a guest.

A typical room in the Sheridan Inn reflects its rich history and offers a cozy, authentic Western experience. The rooms are tastefully decorated with vintage Western touches, including exposed wood beams, antique furniture, and rustic accents. Neutral tones and warm wood paneling create a comfortable, inviting atmosphere. Each room features a plush bed with crisp white linens and a cozy quilt or Western-themed throw blanket.

Ornate, wrought iron, or carved wooden bedframes often enhance the room's historical charm. Period-style furniture such as a wooden dresser, nightstands, and an armchair or rocking chair add to the ambiance.

Some rooms include a writing desk, reflecting a nod to travelers of the Old West.

While the rooms honor the past, they are equipped with modern conveniences like flat-screen televisions, Wi-Fi, and updated bathrooms. Depending on the room, one might enjoy views of the Bighorn Mountains, the historic downtown area, or the hotel's landscaped grounds.

Historical photographs, artwork, or memorabilia related to Buffalo Bill Cody and the Sheridan Inn's storied past. The hotel's commitment to preserving its heritage makes each room feel unique.

Mac got herself settled in and put a framed photograph of her family on her nightstand. It was going to be difficult to get to sleep without Burg by her side and the hustle and bustle of her pre-teens, but she understood that this was for the best for the family now. She was disappointed in herself for allowing matters to get so out of control. For the control freak that she was, it was extremely out of character.

Chapter 10

"*T*his letter you received," John said while talking with Mac on the phone, "have you done anything in response to it?"

"You told me not to," Mac said to John. "I have been busy relocating to a hotel in town. Remember the hotel you stayed in while you were helping me in Sheridan?"

"The Sheridan Inn. I love that place," John said. "I'm sure that Burg feels safer with you and him and the kids staying somewhere other than your house."

"I'm here alone," Mac said.

"Why?"

"Burg kicked me out. He asked for a legal separation," Mac said.

"Oh, Good God," John exclaimed. "That's ridiculous. This too shall pass. My wife and I have hit a few speed bumps over the years. He loves you and the kids and your family. He just overreacted to a bad situation."

"I don't know," Mac said. "He helped me pack."

"My wife threw me out more than once, Mac.

Our jobs are different than most, and spouses sometimes get fed up with the gravity of the crime and the amount of time it takes to solve them.'

"Burg thinks that I choose these crimes over our family," Mac said.

"We sometimes have to, Mac, these are very serious crimes, and they require an exceedingly high level of intellect and time to solve them. They are a complicated jigsaw puzzle, and you are I are good at puzzles."

Mac thought about his explanation for a second before responding. "Burg is right. I have been choosing work over the family for a long time, and he's hit his last nerve of patience with me."

"Like I said, this too shall pass. Just give him a little space and time and he will eventually come around."

"John, I pray that you are right, but it looks bleak from my vantage point."

"Mac, it's part of the package of who we are. Burg has known that about you for as long as he has known you. It is why he was attracted to you in the first place. But I do understand the concept that this is interfering with the family and putting all of you at risk, and Burg is not a risk-taker. You know that. It is part of why you love him. He balances you."

"Back to the letter," Mac said, trying to redirect the focus of the call away from her personal life.

"Not so fast," John said. "In Burg's defense, you promised not to immerse yourself in these crimes which expose your family to dangerous situations.

It wasn't that long ago that you engaged too deeply in The Midnight Scribe Killer and that creep showed up on your doorstep. Burg probably still has PTSD as a result."

"Yes, I know."

"And now you have The Tooth Fairy Killer writing to you at your home. Burg has a good point," John scolded.

"I know."

"Now we can get back to the letter," John said.

"Thank goodness," Mac replied, tired of being reprimanded by every man who meant something to Mac.

Chapter 11

"*I* received another letter," Mac said to John.

"At your house?" Will asked. Both John and Will were at FBI Headquarters brainstorming about Tooth Fairy Killer cases.

"No. At my hotel," Mac said, exasperated. "He knows that I am at the hotel."

"Not good," John said.

"Send it our way," Will said.

"I will. I just got it. It only says three words, "Deny Depose Defend," Mac said.

"That's odd," John admitted. "Everything about this guy is odd."

"That does not align with anything he has done thus far," Will said.

"Agreed. This seems personal, Mac. Please be very careful," John said.

Chapter 12

The crime scene was unbelievable in its staging, timing, and location. A family of three was killed in Gillette, Wyoming in a quaint neighborhood on Lunar Avenue. Lunar Avenue in Gillette is a residential and commercial street located in the northeastern part of the state, within Campbell County. While it is not widely known for specific landmarks, it is representative of Gillette's character as a bustling town shaped by the energy industry and a growing community.

Gillette is often called the "Energy Capital of the Nation" due to its significant coal, oil, and natural gas industries. The town blends its industrial roots with a focus on community living, making it an ideal mix of work opportunities and residential charm. Residents enjoy nearby outdoor activities such as hiking, hunting, and exploring Wyoming's rugged terrain.

Lunar Avenue includes several homes, characterized by Wyoming's mix of modest and modern architecture. Many residences reflect the hardworking ethos of the town's energy workers. Small businesses and services, such as local mechanics, cafes, or family-owned shops are found in the vicinity, as is common in similar areas of Gillette.

As part of a town built on coal-mining wealth, Lunar Avenue is a road connecting various parts of Gillette, often serving as a route for locals heading to work, school, or leisure activities.

The name "Lunar Avenue" evokes celestial imagery such as dreams, isolation, or even cycles of change, resonating with Wyoming's vast, open landscapes and star-filled skies.

In this instance, it is a crime scene of vast imagery. The mother, father, and daughter were found by neighbors after someone had spotted their family cat roaming the neighborhood.

Police reports indicate that all of the mirrors in the house were smashed, the victims each shot once in the head, and all three had their eyeballs removed and replaced with shards of glass from the mirrors. The mother had signs of sexual penetration. All three were staged in the parents' master bedroom, with the parents propped up in bed and the daughter propped sitting on the floor against the bedroom wall facing her parents. It was a bloody scene, and in their blood on the wall above the master bed was scrawled, "Deny Depose Defend."

Mac was sleeping in her hotel room when the call came through from John and Will from FBI headquarters in Washington, D.C.

"Turn on the news," John commanded without introduction or explanation. Mac did as she was told, and immediately she saw the crime scene in Gillette, Wyoming, not more than 90 miles from Sheridan.

"Oh my God," Mac gasped. "The Tooth Fairy Killer is here?"

"Looks like it," Will said.

"That's the same phrase as the letter I received at my hotel yesterday," Mac said. "Turns out that the letter had no stamp or no indication that it was ever mailed. That means that this killer likely hand-delivered it to my hotel."

"I'm calling Burg," John said. "You need a security team with you at all times, Mac. Please be careful."

As Mac hung up her cell phone, she continued to watch the news coverage while making coffee. She felt afraid and alone. She missed her family. She wanted to call Burg but their agreement, according to his terms, was that she had no contact with them.

She poured herself a cup of coffee and started to cry.

Chapter 13

Mac could not watch any more of the news regarding this crime. She couldn't handle the silence in her room and was too terrified to go out for her morning run.   She decided to fill the air with noise and called John back.

"Will and I are en route to the airport to fly to Gillette to investigate this crime," John said.

"I've been thinking about what was written on the wall in blood and what the letter that I received yesterday. Deny, Depose, Defend is a legal strategy used by defense attorneys. The attorney begins the case by systematically denying all allegations against their client, forcing the prosecutor to prove every element of their case. The defense attorney then conducts depositions of witnesses and experts, uncovering discrepancies in the evidence. In court, the defense attorney crafts a compelling narrative, casting doubt on the prosecution's case and undermining the credibility of witnesses," Mac explained.

"The odd thing about the crime scene in Gillette is that there are no bite marks on the victims. The other two Tooth Fairy Killer crime scenes had the bike marks on all victims of the families," John said.

"The fascinating part is the letter he delivered to you and what was written in the victims' blood in Gillette. If you analyze the 'Deny Depose Defend' strategy," Will said, "you get his motive operandi.

The parallel is that the Tooth Fairy Killer 'deposes' his victims psychologically by stalking them, learning their fears, and dismantling their sense of safety before he attacks."

"I think it also resonates with the Tooth Fairy Killer's internal psychology," Mac said. "He denies his own humanity, striving to become the 'Red Dragon' and he deposes his victims by stripping away their identities and seeing them are mere offerings to his delusion. Add to it that he defends his transformation into the Red Dragon, justifying his murders as a necessary step in his evolution."

"Oh, Mac, that is a great analogy. I would not have considered it that way, yet it makes perfect sense," John said. Will agreed. "This is why we need you on our team. You continue to add insight in a way that even professional profilers don't get."

"Thank you. I wish that this sixth sense of mine didn't interfere with my family life," Mac said.

"We know you do," Will agreed.

"We are going to route the plane to Sheridan first and pick you up before we take off for Gillette," John said. "Pack a bag. We are sending a car to pick you up and the driver will remain your bodyguard indefinitely."

"Okay, thanks. I will wait for a call from the front desk upon his arrival," Mac said.

"Yes, don't leave your room until you hear from us who the driver is and he will come up to your room to escort you to the car. He will be brandishing his weapon, so don't be surprised. He has specific instructions from us on how to defend and protect you," John said.

"Okay," Mac agreed, reluctant to leave the safety of her hotel room.

Chapter 13

*J*ohn and Will were near the time of landing in Sheridan to pick Mac up when she got a call from the front desk. She is expecting that it is her bodyguard and driver, ready to get her to the airport, but it is not. It is the front desk informing her that a person in a hoodie and a mask dropped off an envelope for her. She asked that it be delivered to her room and slid under her door.

It read, "My most beautiful treasure and stargazer, I see that you are separated from your family like I once was. I'm sure you are frightened and lonely. I was also frightened and lonely when this happened to me."

Mac was alarmed and confused. She could not understand how this person knew so much about her. She was paranoid enough to think that it could be someone in Burg's family, or worse, the FBI. She was racking her brain as to who could know so much about her when the phone rang again. It was the hotel desk again telling her that a man was there by the name of Brad to take her to the airport. She instructed that he meet her outside of her room.

Within a few minutes, she received a text from John indicating that her bodyguard and driver were named Brad and that it was safe to accompany him in the car to the airport.

Brad was built like a linebacker, and he had the looks of a movie star. He was polite and to the point.

He had a job to do and was engaged by the FBI to protect Mac with his life. He wore a life vest, and a belt with two holsters, and drove a Dodge Ram truck with a gun rack and a Remington on one rung, a Smith and Wesson on the other. He wasn't for show.

Mac was relieved to be in the company of what looked to be a Landman, and it was the first human contact she had had since Burg asked her to leave. She wanted desperately to call Burg, but he had been specific about his requests and demands. She was to have no contact with the family.

Mac arrived at the airport as the FBI jet was landing. The stairs lowered, she entered, the stairs we retracted with her and Brad on the flight, and it promptly took off. Wheels up. It was less than 30 minutes to Gillette, so they didn't have much time to debrief. Mac was quick to show John and Will the letter received at her hotel room within the hour.

"This is personal," John said, looking alarmed and worried. "He knows you."

"Yes. I hate to say this, but I think it is either a family member of Burg or it is someone within the FBI," Mac said.

"So, this guy is psychologically challenging the FBI's unity and your loyalty," Will said. "He's smart.

He knows that planting false leads and creating discord within the investigative team might fracture us. Sounds very much like a Hannibal Lecter move."

"I agree. It's a combo of the Zodiac Killer, the Tooth Fairy Killer, and the Midnight Scribe. Psychological warfare," John said.

"What if we turn it around?" Mac suggested. "What if we try to manipulate the Tooth Fairy Killer using his narcissism and control issues against him?"

"How?" John asked.

"What if I leave him notes at the hotel front desk accusing him of being a lousy copycat and that I see him as a disposable challenging his intellect and calling him a coward for hiding behind his nemesis as a mere copycat," Mac suggested.

"That's dangerous," Will said. "That's putting others at risk, especially you."

"I am already at risk. Every Pollyanna family is at risk," Mac said.

"I'm in," John said.

"I'm in," Will agreed.

They did a three-way hand bump. Mac pulled out her stationery from her room at The Sheridan Inn and started writing.

"Tooth Fairy Want to Be: This is Mary MacIntosh, along with John Douglas and Will Graham. We believe you to be a lousy copycat killer. "

"We will have it messengered back to the hotel," Will said with excitement in his eyes.

Chapter 14

"**W**e need a Mac decoy," Brad said to them as they were landing in Gillette. "Can we send the plane back to Sheridan with a body double of Mac? We need this man to think that she is holed up in her room. That way, we can hopefully garner his attention to appear with another letter. He can then get the letter Mac just wrote. Let's have it be an FBI agent who resembles Mac. She can go out for a morning run and keep Mac's usual schedule. Entrapment 101."

"I like it," John said. "We keep Mac with us, and there can be a dual agent to attract him away from us and to her."

"Exactly," Brad said.

Mac knew that her marriage was likely over. It was her only marriage. Burg had been married before. Divorce was a vocabulary word that he had been throwing around anytime things got tough. Mac was intending to never divorce, but she was pretty sure that Burg had already filed and was requesting full custody. She was confident that Judge Maurita Redle would never grant anything other than shared custody, but she would grant the divorce. Judge Redle was fair and ethical and there was no doubt that Mac and Burg had reached a point of irreconcilable differences. She chose her career first. He chose family.

As they strategized over how to effectuate the body double and to engage the Tooth Fairy Killer into Mac's snare, she noticed how much Brad was fiercely directing for her protection at all costs. Even his own life.

He was strappingly handsome and rugged and strong. She was tall and lean with auburn hair and honey-brown eyes, with long legs and a fine, flat stomach despite giving birth to two sets of twins. Mac felt the energy immediately. She knew that she needed to focus on work and life and family and safety, but she was a hot-blooded woman of 50, and there was a spark.

As the plane descended into Gillette airspace, both John and Will were on their phones making all the arrangements. Brad was calling in favor of a body double. Mac felt defended, accused, vulnerable, afraid, and loved all at the same time.

Chapter 15

$\mathcal{M}$ac created her infamous storyboard at the FBI offices that they rented from the local orthopedic surgeon, Mark G. Murphy of Thunder Basin Orthopedics.

She was convinced who the killer was, but she was reluctant to reveal his name to John, Will, or anyone else. She was aware of the falsely accused people of crime, and she did not want to make a mistake.

Mac had a long transformation into her role with the FBI as a consultant, and she honored her career as both a criminal defense attorney and then a prosecutor, and she had played both sides of the coin. She knew what it was like to defend the falsely accused, and she knew what it was like to prosecute the correctly accused. She knew to be careful with the Tooth Fairy Killer. He was smart and cunning and had Hannibal Lecter as his guidance counselor. The thought of that was terrifying. The smartest serial killer of all time was guiding the Tooth Fairy Killer. It could not be scarier.

Mac was committed and engrossed in this, and she knew that this was her calling in life. It was coming at a high price. She was going to have to find another place to live, endure a divorce, share custody of the kids, and likely go back to work full-time. But this was her calling, and she could not say no.

Chapter 16

The crime scene was one of the worst they had ever seen. The amount of blood was overwhelming, but the gouged-out eye sockets stuffed with shards of broken mirrors were what they could not unsee.

This man was an animal, and the force used to rape the wife and mother was sickening. The entire side of the bed was stained with her blood,

"This is an anger kill," Mac said to the investigatory team. "He hates women."

"He hates good wives and mothers. They represent goodness and kindness that he never had as a child," John added.

"Making the child and husband watch is a statement not to be overlooked," Will noted.

"What do you think that represents?" John asked.

"I think that he is the child making his dad watch something bad happen to his mom," Mac said. "I'm guessing, of course, but nothing else makes sense to me."

"It's highly plausible," John said.

"How is this crime scene alike and how is it different from the Jacobi family in Birmingham, Alabama and the Leeds family in Atlanta?" Mac asked.

She did not travel to either crime scene and so she'd only seen the photos taken by the forensic and law enforcement teams.

"For starters," Will began, "there were more children in the family for both of those."

"And the women were not raped with such force," John added.

"So this is a personal attack on the sanctity and virtuous woman?" Mac asked.

John could see her wheels turning by the sinking look on her face.

"Please don't go there," John said to her. "You are thinking that you have summoned this monster into your life and that this is the scene that was supposed to happen at your house."

"How did you know?" Mac asked him.

"I'm a profiler. I read people for a living."

"With such immediacy and clarity?" Mac asked.

"Yes. Plus I have worked with you a lot over the years, and I know you as a lawyer, profiler, wife, and mother, and you are inserting yourself into this and you are freaking yourself out."

"Well, he obviously stalks people before he kills them, and it is obvious that he's been stalking me, so it is natural to extrapolate where this is going," Mac said.

"You can't let him get into your head, Mac. If you let him in, he wins," Will said.

"He's public enemy number one for all of us. We are a team, and we will defend and protect you," John said assuring her.

"Another difference here is that there are no bite marks," Will continued. "It is my conjecture that Hannibal Lecter somehow advised him to not leave DNA behind."

"How is the forensic dental analysis coming along?" Mac asked.

"Slowly," Will said.

"You should consider using my two forensic dentists. They are in Sheridan, and I used them to help me solve the Rodeo killings. I'll text you their contact information. They are sisters. One is Dr. Michelle Meehan and one is Dr. Kate Meehan Murphy."

"That'd be great. We are struggling with the bite marks. We don't think he ever saw a dentist, although we know he has a cleft palate by the shape of the bite marks," Will said.

"Call Michelle and Kate," Mac said. "They are both very good. The entire family is full of dentists! They truly know teeth. Their dad is a retired dentist. Their brother is a dentist turned orthodontist. Their nephew is a dentist and will be going to orthodontist school. One big happy smiling family!"

"Thanks, I will have the paralegals on the case get in touch with them. We are stuck in the mud on this case. Very few clues. And the fact that Hannibal Lecter is involved in coaching this guy is a huge impediment to solving this. If it wasn't for Will, Hannibal would be a free man. He's excellent at covering up crimes, and I know that he has been consulting with the Tooth Fairy Killer," John said. "We believe that somehow, he takes out personal ads in newspapers using ciphers or codes to communicate with this guy. Hannibal is not allowed to receive unread mail, and he is not allowed to mail anything, but somehow it keeps happening. We aren't too sure that his lawyer is not involved, but we have no proof."

"What does his message on the wall stand for?" Will asked. "Deny, Depose, Defend."

"We spoke of trial strategy," Mac offered, "but in this case, it must go deeper than that. Do we know anything specific about this family and why he chose them?"

"The father is in the oil and gas industry, and the mother is a third-grade teacher at the school that their daughter attends," John said.

"Oil and gas. What specifically does the dad do in the industry?" Mac asked.

"He does frack for methane gas," Will said.

"Fracking. That's what ruined Butch Anderson's ranch in Sheridan years and years ago. It poisoned not only his ranch but also the Powder River that runs through the Sheridan area," Mac said.

"Has he done something recently that was unethical or illegal?" Mac asked. "I would think I would have heard about it if he had done something illegal."

"We are digging into it. We are not sure if he was into something or not. Nothing that has been publicly reported, but our team is at his office now with a search warrant," John said.

"If he was into something bad, these words could have significance to whatever that could be," Mac suggested.

"That's what we are conjecturing as well," John said.

"I need to grab a bite to eat," Mac said. I haven't had anything but coffee today."

"Let's go. The forensic team can wrap this up. Let's get an early dinner and continue this debate downtown. I was told that there is a really good steakhouse downtown," John said. "It's called Wyoming Rib and Chop House and it's not quite downtown but it's not that far away. Everyone says that the food is excellent, and the service is terrific."

They jumped in the car with Mac's new bodyguard driving them to dinner.

Chapter 17

"*T*o surgically correct a cleft palate, a surgeon makes incisions on either side of the cleft in the roof of the mouth, carefully repositions the surrounding tissue and muscles, and then closes the gap with stitches, essentially creating a continuous palate by layering the different tissues such as the mucosa, muscle, and periosteum, to separate the oral and nasal cavities, allowing for proper speech function and eating abilities," Drs. Michelle Meehan and Kate Meehan Murphy said into the speaker phone while at a back booth over a steak dinner. Mac had called both sisters and linked the call so that they could conference about the issue of the cleft lip and the shape of the Tooth Fairy Killer's mouth and teeth.

"If untreated, would the cleft palate affect this man's speech and eating abilities?" Mac asked.

"Yes, it would," Kate said. "He would most likely have a lisp when speaking and difficulty taking a large bite of food."

"He would likely have a crowded mouth, meaning crooked teeth," Michelle chimed in.

"Bingo," Will said. "This guy definitely has a narrow jaw and crooked teeth from the analysis of the bite marks left on some of the victims."

"We find it odd that he didn't bite the Gillette victims since this seemed to be his signature or pattern with the two other families on the East Coast," Michelle said.

"We are considering a copycat killer," John admitted. "This one feels a little different, but we are unsure about it."

"We don't know how much the FBI knows about crime in Wyoming," Kate said, "but it remains rare. Violent crime is extremely rare because most people own a gun."

"However, since our serial killer during The Sheridan WYO Rodeo, we certainly have had a tremendous uptick in violent crime," Mac offered. "We have the Red Hands Missing and Murdered Indigenous Women, we had the Dating Game Killer, Prison Break-related crime, DB Cooper, and the Pumpkin Buttes. Things have definitely changed around here."

"Yes, but most of the killers are not from Wyoming. They have ventured to remote parts of the country where it is less likely to get caught," John said.

"Most of these people have been caught, thanks to Mac and law enforcement in this state," Will said.

"We still have no grip on the Red Hands crimes against Native American women," Michelle said. "We continue to hear of these cases regularly. It is truly disheartening. Many of us have Native American friends, clients, patients, and co-workers."

"The FBI has been complicit in this," Kate said. "It is time that you stepped up your game in law enforcement."

Will and John looked at each other over the dinner table. They both nodded their heads. She was not incorrect.

"We agree," Will said into the speakerphone. "Mac has made us readily aware of this."

"We thank you, ladies, for giving us your time. The FBI profiling team is putting together a file for your review and consideration, and we thank you for agreeing to assist us with the forensic analysis of the teeth marks for the Alabama and Georgia open cases," John said.

"It is our pleasure to help. Mac is a friend of ours and Sheridan has been lucky to have her as our former prosecutor and now our neighbor. Our kids go to school together," Michelle said.

"Speaking of," Kate interjected, we have not seen you at drop off or pick up or at any of the sporting events. Is everything alright?"

Mac gulped back a breath. "No. It's not. Burg and I are separated.   It's a long story and I don't know how it will resolve," she admitted. "I'm praying that we can work things out, but right now he's asked me to move out and stay away and given him and the children space. It's not good."

"I'm sorry to hear this," Michelle said. "Marriage is tough enough, and then we professional women add our careers into the mix, and there can be plenty of complications."

"We understand," Kate said empathetically.

"Thank you. I appreciate the support and please keep this to yourselves. I don't want to live in a fishbowl and be the gossip of the school," Mac said.

"Understood," both sisters said in unison before they ended the call.

Chapter 18

*M*ac was an expert in fracking, as she represented Butch Anderson in his fracking case that ruined his ranch and his business years back in Sheridan. She explained it to Will and John in their spare hotel room that they were using as their meeting room for the case.

"Fracking, or hydraulic fracturing, is a technique used to extract oil and natural gas from underground rock formations, particularly shale. The process involves injecting a mixture of water sand, and chemicals at high pressure into the rock to create fractures. These fractures allow oil and gas to flow more freely and be collected," Mac said.

"Do they use a large drill?" John asked.

"Yes. A well is drilled vertically into the earth and often horizontally through the sale layers. The pressurized mixture is pumped into the well creating fissures in the rocks, allowing oil or gas to flow through these fissures into the well and is brought to the surface," she explained.

"Does it harm the environment?" Will asked.

"Yes, because they use millions of gallons of water, mixed with potentially toxic chemicals, which may leak into the groundwater supplies. Spills or improper disposal of wastewater can pollute drinking water."

"What about the air?" Will asked.

"Methane, a potent greenhouse gas, can escape during the extraction process, contributing to climate change. Also, the fracking sites also emit volatile organic compounds leading to smog and respiratory issues. It can also increase seismic activity, causing small earthquakes in areas not typically prone to them."

"I'm surprised that a state like pristine Wyoming would allow that," Will said.

"It is controversial," Mac admitted. "But it also employs a lot of people,"

"This couple that was killed, are they somehow linked to fracking and toxins in the water?" John asked.

"Yes, it turns out that our paralegals just sent over an email with the names of two landowners in the Pavillion area near Gillette who sued a company called Encana for withholding information about water quality and contamination. The case is still pending here," Will said while reading an email off his laptop.

"Who owns or operates Encana?" Mac asked.

I will keep reading from the paralegal's research. "Turns out that Brent Cracken is the President and CEO of Encana, and he is our murder victim. His wife, Cindy is the schoolteacher, and their daughter, Wendy was the student at Cindy's school."

"Now we are getting somewhere," Mac said.

"Yes, this man was likely murdered for raping the land here, and the killer, in turn, aggressively attacked his wife," John said.

"I feel more and more like this is a copycat killer," Will said. "Similar M.O., but motivation seems directed at the husband, and there are no teeth marks as a signature of the Tooth Fairy Killer."

"I tend to agree, but why send me the letters?" Mac asked. "The only tie I have to fracking is the case I handled over a decade ago for Butch Anderson and the fracking incident on his ranch. I have no ties to anything in the energy business and no ties to Gillette."

"It could be the fracking case," John said. "There aren't a lot of large jury verdicts around here surrounding that and you obtained one."

"True," Mac admitted. "But that was so long ago. One would have needed to know about it. No one talks about it anymore in these parts. I have not had it raised in years."

"The killer in this case knows something about you to send you two letters and they seem to be personal, about you and your personal life," John said.

"Agreed, but why link me to this killing? Especially if it is a copycat?"

"That is the million-dollar question," John said.

Chapter 20

*M*ac was exhausted and retired to her room, but her head was still spinning. She was envisioning her storyboard and the missing links. She pulled out her cell and started searching for lunar cycles in the Sheridan/Gillette area over the last few days and was surprised to see those two nights prior was a blood moon and that in only two days' time, it was back to a normal moonlight tonight. She thought of the symbolism in that concept, and she thought that it mirrored her journey often from chaos to clarity, whether it be in her cases as a defense attorney, prosecutor, profiler, mother, or wife.

The red light of the blood moon was when the Gillette murders took place, which was a haunting reminder of the killer's delusions, and the lives destroyed.

Mac turned on soft music, turned down the covers, and crawled into bed. Her bathroom nightlight set off a soft glow, and with the dimmed lights, soft music, dark room, and sheer exhaustion, Mac fell into a deep sleep.

Chapter 21

Mac awoke to the sound of her alarm, and quickly made coffee, brushed her teeth, and laced up her shoes before heading out for her morning run. She spoke with her bodyguard the night prior, and he agreed to accompany her on an early morning run. He promptly met her at the elevator, and they headed out into the crisp morning air for some exercise.

At first, he didn't talk much, but as they warmed up, he started becoming more chatty. He knew a lot about her, but she did not know a lot about him.

Brad explained that he was a Navy Seal and trained for combat, but post-retirement, he took a job as a bodyguard and made a lot more money than he did in the military. He was very fit, handsome, and smart, and he could articulate about nearly any subject. He was very well-traveled and spoke three languages. She was intrigued.

When they returned from their run, John and Will were awaiting them in the lobby. John spoke first.

"The Great Red Dragon and the Woman Clothes in Sun painting has been stolen from the Baltimore Museum," John said.

The painting that this killer is obsessed with?" Mac asked. The oil pained by William Blake around 1805 regarding the Book of Revelation?"

"Yes," John said.

They had all been briefed that this painting visually represented imagery of cosmic battles between good and evil, with the ultimate victory of God's forces over Satan. The woman represented the Church, Israel, or Mary, depending on the interpretation. Clothed in the sun, with a crown of twelve stars and the moon under her feet, depicted purity, divine protection, and God's chosen people. The woman is pregnant and about to give birth which symbolizes the arrival of Christ or the birth of a new spiritual era. The dragon represented Satan, described in Revelation as a seven-headed, ten-horned beast with a tail that swept one-third of the canvas to the stars in the sky. The dragon was waiting to devour the child, symbolizing Satan's attempt to destroy Christ or undermine God's plan.

The painting captured the epic spiritual warfare between the forces of God and the forces of evil. The child, traditionally interpreted as Jesus, was destined to rule all nations but was protected by God and taken to safety. It represented the struggle between divine forces and demonic forces. The woman symbolizes God's faithful people under attack by Satan. The dragon's attempt to devour her child shows Satan's ongoing opposition to God's plans of salvation and his hostility toward Christ.

Ultimately, the scene emphasizes God's triumph over evil. The child is protected, and Revelation foretells the dragon's ultimate defeat, symbolizing the victory of righteousness over sin and chaos.

Its depiction intensifies the drama and spiritual tension of the vision, highlighting humanity's role in the cosmic battle and God's promises of salvation.

"How in the world could that precious piece of art get stolen? Isn't under lock and key like the Mona Lisa?" Mac asked.

"Whoever did this, knew what they were doing. No alarm was set off. Not a trace of an entrance. It's like the cat burglar was there," John said.

"We all know that the Tooth Fairy Killer is absolutely obsessed with this painting and believes that he is the Red Dragon in that painting," Mac said. "That means if it is the real Tooth Fairy Killer, he was on the East Coast this morning, which means that he never left the East Coast and we are dealing with a copycat, or the real McCoy is able to freely travel without detection, and swiftly."

Chapter 22

*T*hey watched the news coverage together in their "war room" of their hotel, noting that the museum had never experienced a theft, but showed the video footage of the man stealing the priceless piece of art. He was tall, with a hoodie, and when he turned to leave holding the large painting, one could clearly see his cleft lip.

Mac turned to John and Will. "We have a problem. This is the real Tooth Fairy Killer, and he is on the East Coast. I am now convinced that what happened in Gillette must be a copycat killer. The motive is different. The personal notes to me are different. The message above the headboard is different. Now we need to triage and determine who goes after the Tooth Fairy Killer and who tracks down the copycat," she said.

"Agreed," John said. "But we will stay here with you on this one and hopefully solve it before we pivot to the East Coast. This one should be solvable. I think this is a message to you, Mac."

"Who would want to scare me or commit a crime to frighten me? I just can't pin this one down. Burg is plenty upset with me, but he is not a criminal. I don't have any other enemies that I am aware of," Mac said.

"Mac, be real. How many people have you prosecuted and put behind bars? The list is endless," John said.

"You have a good point. I have put a lot of people behind bars. I guess one of them could be seeking revenge," Mac said.

"Pinning it down won't be easy," Will chimed in.

"It could have nothing to do with your career. It could be a scorned lover from the past or someone who simply doesn't like you," John suggested. "You are a very successful and powerful woman, and you intimidate people."

"I don't try to. I just live my life," Mac said in defense.

"Ironman Triathlon, multiple marathons including Boston, law school, defense lawyer, prosecutor, wife, mother, etc. There are a lot of these things that add up to people being either in awe of you or intimidated by you," John continued.

Mac had a habit of avoiding self-reflection, and she did not see her accomplishments the same way others might. She liked to challenge herself. She was not trying to intimidate others, but the guys could be onto something.

"Well, rather than try to create a laundry list of who might be this copycat killer here in Gillette, we need to look at the evidence and try to determine who this person is before they kill again," Mac suggested.

They both nodded and rolled up their sleeves. It was time to get to work.

Chapter 23

"*I* think we need to host a news conference and publicly announce our theory that this situation in Gillette is that of a copycat killer, and either way, we trap the Tooth Fairy Killer into a challenge that someone could copy him, or, if we are correct in that this is a copycat, then the perpetrator will know that we know that he's not the real deal," Mac said to John and Will after shifting through the evidence and separating then two different motives.

"Good idea," John said.

"The two glaring differences consist of a different staging of a crime scene and the fact that the CEO of this fracking company seemed to be the true target, not the wife of the house. She is a working mom, unlike the East Coast cases where the wife is the June Cleaver of the household. In this case, the husband is the controversial one who seems to be involved in corrupt business practices," Mac continued.

"If we can announce our theory and make this publicly available on the global networks, we will target a large number of viewers," Will said.

"I'll set it up with the FBI," John said.

Chapter 24

"The news conference was well received," Will said. "I think we got the message out because the FBI team in D.C. got a lot of new tips on the theft of the painting."

People called in about the painting and how valuable it was both religiously and symbolically, and there was a public outcry as to how it could have been stolen and why.

Theories ranged all over the map, but the most common theory was that the Tooth Fairy Killer was the culprit, leading to tips as to where this man was and possibly who he was.

There had been another "add" taken out in the Tattler and it was believed now that it was a cipher from no other than Hannibal Lecter to the Tooth Fairy Killer giving the killer the address of Will Graham's home in Florida with instructions to kill Will. Will was the FBI profiler who caught Hannibal Lecter, and it was Lecter's revenge to kill Will in front of his family in their family home. The cipher in the newspaper was Hannibal's work, telling the Tooth Fairy Killer Will's address with specific instructions on how to kill Will's family. The crime scene was to mirror that of the Jacobi family in Birmingham, Alabama and the Leeds family in Atlanta, Georgia.

"Hannibal delights in manipulating others, particularly those investigating him or seeking his help," Will said to Mac and John.

"Communicating and directing the Tooth Fairy Killer covertly demonstrates his brilliance and the failure of the institution to fully contain his influence."

"Why are you the Tooth Fairy target?" Mac asked.

"I'm not his target, I am Hannibal's target, and Hannibal is using Tooth Fairy manipulatively to seek revenge on me for catching him," Will said. "It shows the power of manipulating, the fragility of the justice system, the psychological thrill of the cat-and-mouse game, Hannibal Lecter's personal obsession with me, raising the stakes with a calculated hit on my family, his ability to confront me even from prison, the power of foreboding, transformation, and symbolism of use of the blood moon and the crescent moon, combined with the painting of The Great Red Dragon and the Woman Clothed in Sun," Will said.

"So, all of these have merged with The Tooth Fairy Killer likely stole the painting in Baltimore," Mac said.

"Yes," Will agreed.

"It is coming to a head," John said. If this killer stole the painting, he likely did it not only to please himself and show his strength in manipulation, but he did it to prove himself worthy of Hannibal.

"Exactly," Will said.

Will's cell phone rang. It was FBI headquarters calling to tell him that they think that the Tooth Fairy Killer was the thief based on surveillance cameras throughout the city of Baltimore, and they think that they have pinpointed where the killer lives. The FBI was on their way to his apartment in downtown Baltimore as they spoke.

"Turn on the news," Will said. Mac did as instructed. "Live on all major networks was the FBI and Swat teams surrounding an apartment building in downtown Baltimore with guns drawn. There were reports that the FBI and Swat broke down his door and caught him in the middle of eating the painting.

Chapter 25

*T*here was a great sense of relief when the Tooth Fairy Killer was caught, but he wasn't taken into custody because he fought back and was shot multiple times by the Swat team. He was dead, and so was Hannibal Lecter's ability to manipulate this man with the cleft lip.

This gave Will Graham a great sense of relief. Hannibal remained behind bars and was no longer allowed any privileges of communication unless it was with his lawyers, who were not allowed to transport anything into or out of the prison.

The killer was identified as Francis Dolarhyde. He was gone.

Chapter 26

"**W**ith the Tooth Fairy Killer case solved, we can pivot back to this murder in Gillette," Mac said.

It's obvious that it is a copycat at this point, so now we need to focus on who this might be," John said.

"I'm glad that Will was able to fly home to Florida to see his family. He needed a break after Dolarhyde was caught and killed, and he needs to get Hannibal Lecter out of his mind for a while," Mac said.

"Agreed. It's been a long, stressful set of events not only for Will but for his family," John said.

"Do you think that he will stay put in retirement?" Mac asked.

"I do. His wife insists," John said. "She deserves him to be home with her and their son."

The phone in their hotel room rang. It was the front desk. Someone had dropped an envelope off for delivery to Mary MacIntosh. John said that he would go down and get it. Mac was to stay put in the room.

Chapter 27

*J*ohn opened the letter and handed it to Mac. It read:

"I'm returning to you the journal you kept as a little girl, and I will have your telescope shipped to your hotel. I don't think you remember me, but I've always remembered you. You'll see me soon. You will understand shy it has to be you."

John pulled a brown leather-bound journal from the envelope and handed it to Mac. "Is this your journal?" John asked.

"It is. It was stolen from the house that my mom and I lived in. We had a break-in, and the only things taken were my telescope and my journal," Mac said.

"Who do you think broke into your house?" John asked.

"My dad."

"Why would he do that?"

"Because my mom divorced him and got full custody, and I was not allowed to contact my dad in any form. He was not a good guy. The only nice things he did with me were astrology and encouraging me to journal about the moon and the stars. He bought me the telescope," Mac said.

"So, you think that your dad could be the copycat killer?" John asked incredulously.

"I don't know. He has been a career criminal his entire life, but I don't know if he is capable of murder!"

"That's extreme, I admit, but he's obviously seeking your attention, and your attention has been on the Tooth Fairy Killer for a while. I guess it might make sense," John said.

Mac sat on the bed and flipped through her journal. She had written about celestial cycles and drawn pictures of constellations and moon cycles, highly focused on the crescent moon. It was like a walk down memory lane. John could see tears welling in her eyes. He sat down next to her and put his arm around her shoulder in a fatherly fashion.

"It's going to be okay, Mac. Even if it is him, it's going to be okay," John said.

Mac let the tears flow.

Chapter 28

*T*he front desk called again within the hour indicating that another envelope had been delivered addressed to Mary MacIntosh. John went to retrieve it. He opened it and it read:

"By now, you have seen the map and you've seen the photos. You know this is all about you. But have you figured out why? If not, don't worry – I'll give you time. After all, the game is just beginning. And you love puzzles and games."

John handed her a map and some photos.

"This is a map from our hotel to the Lunar Avenue crime scene," Mac said to John. She handed him the map. And then her eyes flew wide open when she looked at the photos. "These are pictures of the crime scene?"

She handed them to him, and he looked a them, shaking his head. They were of the parents dead in bed and the daughter posed across the room with her eyes gouged out and replaced with mirrors.

"Your dad is the copycat killer," John said to her.

"He is. These poor people lost their lives all to allow my dad to have my attention. I feel ill," Mac said.

"There's more." John handed her a map with a pin in it. "It is pinning the Crescent Sky Observatory on the hill above Gillette. It is an invitation for you to meet him there," John said.

"Not in my life am I going to meet him there," Mac said.

"We need to, Mac. It's the only way we stop this. We will have the FBI and the Swat and local law enforcement with us. I will dress as an FBI agent to look like you as a body double. You can stay safely in the van. But you will have to be wired with a bug in your ear so that you can direct the female agent as to what to say to him. He has to believe that it is you."

"What if something goes wrong?"

"We are the FBI. We know how to do this. Trust us," John said.

While he was making calls and summoning teams, Mac decided that it was time to reach out to Burg. She had given him sufficient time and space, but this was very serious, and he needed to be in the loop.

She explained what was going down to her husband, and he was mortified for her and apologetic. He had kicked his wife out of their home and out of the family, only to learn that this was a direct target on Mac by her father – a lifelong thug and criminal and someone she had no contact with since she was a little girl. He felt guilty and terrible, and he told her so.

She explained the plan and that she would remain in the van safely, but that they needed to set this trap and catch her father before he was killed again.

Burg agreed with the plan, but not without profusely apologizing to her.

Chapter 29

*T*he Crescent Sky Observatory was an abandoned building on the outskirts of town, and Mac could hear John and the female FBI agent talk to each other describing what they were experiencing.

John said deliberately into the microphone wired to his chest, "It is damp in here and it carries the tainted smell of mildew."

The female agent replied, "With the help of this flashlight I can see overturned furniture, old equipment, and graffiti scrawled on the walls. But what my eyes are focusing on is in the middle of the room. I see a single desk, clean and carefully arranged, and I think I see a letter addressed to me. Next to the desk is my childhood telescope."

Mac could picture what this scene looked like.

The agent stepped forward and reached for the envelope.

"Careful," John said to her.

"I know," she replied, reading the letter aloud.

"Do you remember this place? You should – it's where everything began. But if you've forgotten, don't worry. I've left a reminder for you. The stars told me we'd meet here again, under the light.

You always loved the stars, didn't you? So did I. But while you saw beauty, I saw the truth – they burn so brightly because they're dying. Just like we all are. If you truly want to understand, you'll need to look back. Go to the place where the crescent moon first appeared in your life. Only then will you see why I chose you."

Mac spoke into her headset that both John and the female FBI agent were wired to.

"The crescent moon," Mac said aloud for the female agent to repeat.

"What is it?" John asked the agent, so as to relay this to Mac.

Mac continued, "When I was a little girl, I used to come here with my father. He was an amateur astronomer. We'd watch the stars, and he'd always talk about the crescent moon being a symbol of something unfinished. He said it was like life – always in progress, never whole." The agent repeated Mac's words.

"You think this is about your father," John said in an obvious manner, acting as if they were only just suspecting this.

Mac instructed the female agent to pivot to the telescope. And then she instructed the agent to say, "No, it's more than that." Mac instructed her to extend the telescope, revealing an engraving at the base. Mac said aloud what she remembered being engraved. "It's my initials and his initials."

John looked closely and saw their initials engraved with a heart symbol in the middle. John deliberately said out loud, "MM heart GM," is the engraving.

"Yes, it was her way of telling me he loved me," Mac said into the microphone to be repeated.

Then they both heard the sound of shuffling feet and Mac could hear panic in John's voice.

"Don't move," John said to the shadow.

Mac heard gunfire. And then silence.

Chapter 30

$\mathcal{M}$ac watched from the van as John and the female agent emerged from the observatory. She knew that it was over. Her father had been shot and killed. The sense of relief was indescribable.

After the forensics were done with the scene and Mac had time to debrief with the FBI team, she spoke with them about the moral complexity of the motive. Her dad never liked the raping and pillaging of the land by the oil, gas and coal mining companies, and she grappled with her father's motive to stop illegal fracking, as it presented a twisted form of vigilante justice. She also spoke of her personal connection between the killer and his betrayal, and she explained that this would have a ripple effect on her career, family, and psyche. She explained how she felt that this was rocking her world, and how it had strained her marriage, causing her husband to push her away, underscoring the devastating impact of betrayal and guilt.

Mac knew that Burg's realization of the truth and his regret for how he had handled things would make reuniting a vulnerable moment for their family but offering a chance at reconciliation. Mac reflected on her feelings of isolation from her husband and children and her desperate need to be a family again.

Upon further reflection, she felt that this mirrored the psychological toll of her father's actions, pushing her to explore her inner strength to make difficult choices regarding reconciliation, and how they would navigate heartbreak, guilt, and forgiveness.

Burg had struggled with understanding her intense focus on the Tooth Fairy Killer case, but when he learned the truth, his guilt was overwhelming. He would do anything within his power to win her back, but he admitted to her that he was paralyzed with shame, and this interfered with how she saw him as a father and a husband. She knew that their relationship would never be the same. There were lingering trust issues, and Mac knew that she would likely never allow Burg fully back into her heart.

She knew that the combination of her father's betrayal and her husband's initial rejection was going to make her journey all the more challenging. If they did reconcile, it would be bittersweet, but it should combine with strength of love and forgiveness, carrying with it the weight of what had transpired.

She told John before they parted ways that she would have to give it some time before deciding what to do, she had decided to stay at The Sheridan Inn a little longer, but that she would see the children right away. They missed their mom. She missed her four children in the worst way.